E 3
ROB

D1301022

Fibonacci Zoo

by Tom Robinson   illustrated by Christina Wald

Today was a special day for Eli and his father. They were going to visit the Fibonacci Zoo. His teacher said it was different from most zoos and Eli couldn't wait to find out why. He brought a notebook to record what he saw.

Eli entered the zoo and saw an alligator swimming in a shallow lake. He looked around for others but there were none. He pulled out his notebook and wrote: "1 alligator."

Leaving the alligator, he discovered a bison out sunning himself. Again Eli looked but he could see only one. In his notebook, he wrote: "1 bison."

$$1 = 1$$
$$1 \quad 1$$

Eli wondered why there were so few animals in this
zoo. He and his father left the bison and saw two
hairy camels standing near a pond. Eli knew they
were camels because of the humps on their backs.
He added a new entry: "2 camels."

Next they found a tank of water. The animals inside were swimming and jumping into the air. When all three soared above the wall, Eli recognized the dolphins. Eli and his father moved on, but not before he made a new entry in his notebook: "3 dolphins."

$$1 + 2 = 3$$

1   1   2   3

After a short walk through some trees, Eli and his father saw five large creatures. They moved in a familiar way. They swished their tails and swung their trunks. These were elephants. Eli made his next entry: "5 elephants."

2 + 3 = 5

1　1　2　3　5

Soon tall pink birds stood on long legs. Eli recognized flamingos and quickly counted eight of them. In his notebook he recorded "8 flamingos."

camels
dolphins
5 elephants
8 flami

$$3 + 5 = 8$$

1 1 2 3 5 8

"Hey, Dad, look at this!" Eli exclaimed. "I've been keeping track of the animals we've seen. We saw 1 alligator, 1 bison, 2 camels, 3 dolphins, 5 elephants, and now 8 flamingos. I think there's a pattern. If I take any two numbers in order and add them up, I get the next number."

1 alligator   **1 bison**   **2 camels**

3 dolphins   **5 elephants**

8 flamingos

"See? 1 + 1 = 2. 1 + 2 = 3. 2 + 3 = 5. And 3 + 5 = 8. If this keeps up, I bet we'll find 5 + 8 = 13 animals next!"

"Come on," called his father. "Let's find out!"

They heard the next group of animals long before they reached them. Sitting under some trees were thirteen gorillas.

"Exactly thirteen. Just like I thought!" shouted Eli. He made an entry in his notebook: "13 gorillas."

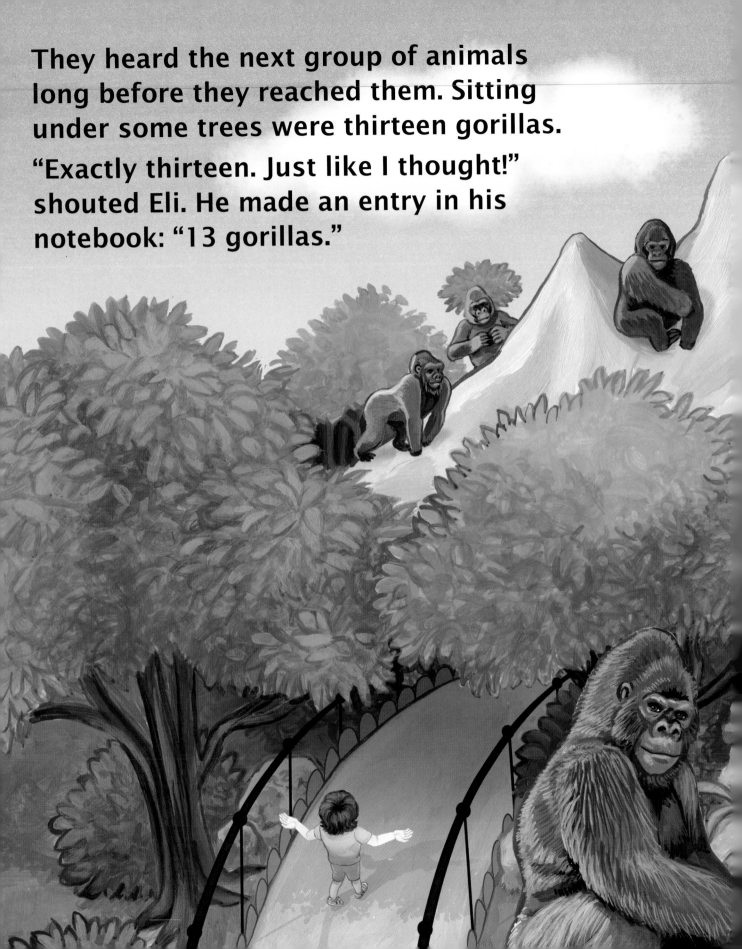

$$5 + 8 = 13$$

1 1 2 3 5 8 13

Looking in his notebook, Eli saw that the next exhibit should contain twenty-one animals. He was right. Twenty-one enormous creatures lay in a shallow pond. This was the hippopotamus exhibit. Eli pulled out his notebook one more time and wrote: "21 hippos."

$$8 + 13 = 21$$

1   1   2   3   5   8   13   21

This was an unusual zoo. Eli enjoyed the animals he saw. He had discovered the secret of the Fibonacci Zoo. He couldn't wait to see how many animals would be in its next exhibit.

Can you guess?

13+21= ?

1 1 2 3 5 8 13 21

For Creative Minds

Number Patterns

A number pattern is a list of numbers that follows a particular sequence.

When a number pattern is made by skip counting, it is an **arithmetic sequence**. For example, "5, 10, 15, 20," is an arithmetic sequence. This sequence is made by skip counting with fives. The number you skip count by—in this case, 5—is called the common difference.

Some number patterns use multiplication to find the next number. This is called a **geometric sequence**. For example, "1, 3, 9, 27" is a geometric sequence. Each number is the product of 3 and the previous number.

There are other kinds of number patterns that are not arithmetic or geometric patterns. One example is the pattern Eli discovers in the zoo: the Fibonacci sequence. A mathematician named Leonardo Pisano (whose nickname was Fibonacci) first discovered this number pattern in the year 1202. The Fibonacci sequence begins with the number 1. Each number in the pattern is the sum of the previous two numbers.

Look at the number patterns below. Match each number pattern to its description. Then fill in the missing number.

A. 1, 2, 4, __, 16, 32, 64 . . .

B. 0, 7, 14, 21, 28, 35, __ . . .

C. __, 2, 3, 4, 5, 6, 7, 8 . . .

D. 2, 4, 6, 8, __, 12, 14 . . .

E. 1, 3, 5, __, 9, 11, 13 . . .

1. This is a number pattern of even numbers, made by skip counting with 2s.
2. This is a number pattern of odd numbers, starting with 1 and skip counting by 2s.
3. In this geometric pattern, each number is double (two times) the previous number.
4. In this arithmetic sequence, the common difference is 1.
5. In this arithmetic sequence, the common difference is 7.

Match to the description: A-3, B-5, C-4, D-1, E-2.
Missing number: A-8, B-42, C-1, D-10, E-7

Fibonacci Numbers in Nature

The numbers of the Fibonacci sequence often appear in nature. Count the number of petals on a flower, the number of leaves on a twig, or the number of seeds in an apple. You might find a Fibonacci number! Many plants—but not all—have a general tendency to grow leaves or petals that match a Fibonacci number. Even in plants that usually have a Fibonacci number, there can be individual plants that grow differently. For example, most clovers have 3 leaves. But sometimes a clover grows an extra leaf and is a lucky four-leaf clover! Sometimes a flower might have one petal that is stunted or torn off.

Count the petals or leaves of the plants below and see how many are Fibonacci numbers.

Answer: All of them!

Fibonacci and You

The Fibonacci numbers appear in the human body! Humans have 5 appendages off the trunk of the body: 1 head, 2 arms, and 2 legs. We have 2 arms. Each arm has 3 parts: upper arm, forearm, and hand. Each hand has 5 fingers. Where else can you find Fibonacci numbers?

Golden Spiral

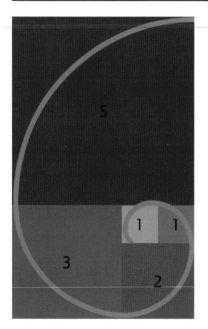

The Fibonacci sequence can be used to create a spiral. Begin with the 1 square inside. If you trace from corner to corner on each square, you will see a spiral pattern. This pattern can continue forever, adding bigger and bigger squares.

galaxy

hurricane

This spiral often appears in nature and is called the **golden spiral**. This is the shape of spiral galaxies in space. This is the spiral of hurricanes moving across the ocean.

Look at the images below to see other examples of the golden spiral in nature.

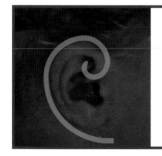

Fibonacci and You

The golden spiral can be found in the human body too! It is in the curve of our ears and the swirl in our closed hands.

Animal Matching

Match the description of each animal to the name and picture on the left. Answers are below.

A. This large reptile is covered in small, bony scales. When it rests in the water, this animal looks like a log or part of a tree. This animal is native to North America and Asia.

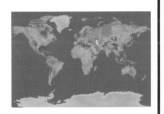

camel

B. This mammal is the largest land animal in North America. It weighs up to 2,800 pounds (1270 kg). This animal is often confused with its African relative, the buffalo, but they are different species.

gorilla

C. This mammal is known for the humps on its back. Some have only one hump and are found in Africa and the Middle East. Others have two humps and are native to central Asia.

alligator

D. This mammal uses tools to find food, cross rivers, and build nests. It can use sign language to talk with humans. This animal is native to Africa.

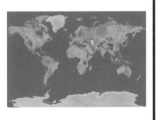

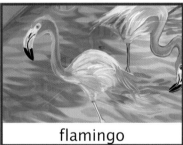

flamingo

E. This bird likes to stand on one leg. Most of these animals live in South America or Africa. They can also be found in North America, Asia, and Europe.

bison

For Lisa, my inspiration—TR

To the Cincinnati Zoo, one of my favorite places to sketch, even if it is not a Fibonacci—CW

Thanks to Dr. James Wilson, Professor of Mathematics Education at the University of Georgia, and to Karen Mitchell, elementary teacher from Smyrna, GA, for reviewing the accuracy of the information in this book.

Thanks to the following photographers for releasing their images into the public domain (in order of appearance): Lynn Greyling: gardenia leaves, Maliz Ong: wild calla lily, Alison Breskin: tree leaves, Maliz Ong: kalachuchi flower, Josef Petrek: apple blossom, Maliz Ong: Flower, ESA/Hubble & NASA: spiral galaxy, Tim Loomis (NOAA/NESDIS/Environmental Visualization Program): hurricane, Carlos Sardá: ram horn, Rostislav Kralik: plant spiral, Lisa McCarty: seahorse, Lesley Huntley: fern frond.
Thanks to Zoomdak Photography (www.zoomdak.com) for the photo of author Tom Robinson.
Arbordale Publishing: human ear and hand

Library of Congress Cataloging-in-Publication Data

Robinson, Tom, (Tom Mark), 1968-
 Fibonacci Zoo / by Tom Robinson ; illustrated by Christina Wald.
   pages cm
 Summary: When Eli and his father visit an unusual zoo, Eli keeps track of the numbers of animals and soon sees there is a pattern that will predict how many creatures are in the next exhibit. Includes an activity and facts about number sequences.
 ISBN 978-1-62855-553-0 (English hardcover) -- ISBN 978-1-62855-562-2 (English pbk.) -- ISBN 978-1-62855-580-6 (English downloadable ebook) -- ISBN 978-1-62855-598-1 (English interactive dual-language ebook) -- ISBN 978-1-62855-571-4 (Spanish pbk.) -- ISBN 978-1-62855-589-9 (Spanish downloadable ebook) -- ISBN 978-1-62855-607-0 (Spanish interactive dual-language ebook) [1. Zoos--Fiction. 2. Fibonacci numbers--Fiction. 3. Sequences (Mathematics)--Fiction.] I. Wald, Christina, illustrator. II. Title.
 PZ7.R62Fib 2015
 [E]--dc23
                    2014037417

Translated into Spanish: *El zoológico Fibonacci*
Lexile® Level: 510L
key phrases for educators: number patterns, fibonacci, counting, addition, skip-counting, zoo animals

Bibliography:

Animals. National Geographic. Web. Accessed 2014.
Campbell, Sarah and Campbell, Richard. Growing Patterns: Fibonacci Numbers in Nature. Boyds Mills, 2010. Print.
D'Agnese, Joseph. Blockhead: The Life of Fibonacci. Henry Holt and Co., 2010. Print
Garland, Trudi Hammel and Gage, Rachel. Fibonacci Fun: Fascinating Activities With Intriguing Numbers. Dale Seymour, 1997. Print.
Garland, Trudi Hammel. Fascinating Fibonaccis. Dale Seymour, 1990. Print.
Hulme, Joy and Schwartz, Carol. Wild Fibonacci: Nature's Secret Code Revealed. Tricycle Press, 2005. Print.
Komiya, Teruyuki, et al. Life-Size Zoo: From Tiny Rodents to Gigantic Elephants, An Actual Size Animal Encyclopedia. Seven Footer, 2009. Print.
Sigler, Laurence. Fibonacci's Liber Abaci: A Translation into Modern English of Leonardo Pisano's Book of Calculation. Springer, 2003. Print.
Spelman, Lucy. National Geographic Animal Encyclopedia: 2,500 Animals with Photos, Maps and More! National Geographic Children's Books, 2012. Print.

Manufactured in China, January 2015
This product conforms to CPSIA 2008
First Printing

Arbordale Publishing
Mt. Pleasant, SC 29464
www.ArbordalePublishing.com